Pants for Chuck

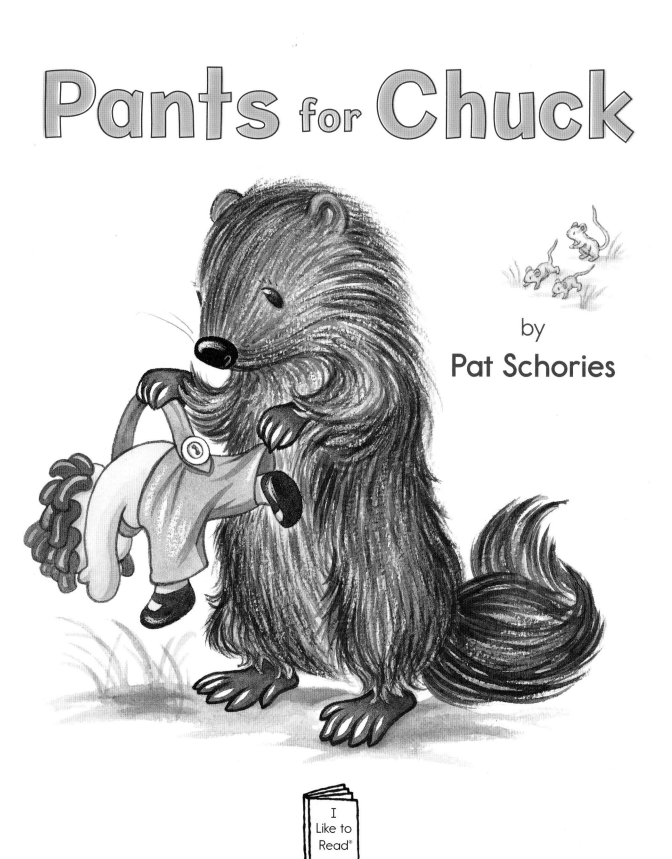

by
Pat Schories

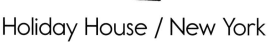

Holiday House / New York

*For Barbara, my good friend
and old neighbor*

Printed and Bound in March 2014 at Tien Wah Press, Johor Bahru, Johor, Malaysia.
The artwork was created with watercolors on Arches Cold Press paper.
Some digital manipulations were made to the final scans, particularly for the endpapers.
www.holidayhouse.com
First Edition
1 3 5 7 9 10 8 6 4 2

Library of Congress Cataloging-in-Publication Data
Schories, Pat, author, illustrator.
Pants for Chuck / by Pat Schories. — First edition.
pages cm. — (I like to read)
Summary: Chuck's friends encourage him to join them in running, climbing, and
playing, but Chuck is wearing pants that are a bit too small.
ISBN 978-0-8234-3066-6 (hardcover)
[1. Play—Fiction. 2. Pants—Fiction. 3. Woodchuck—Fiction.] I. Title.
PZ7.S37645Pan 2014
[E]—dc23
2013037254

Play with us, Big Chuck.

Run with us, Big Chuck!

Climb with us, Big Chuck!

What do you see, Chuck?

What are you doing?

Those pants are too small, Chuck.

You are too big,
and the pants are too small.

Come on, Big Chuck.
Run with us.

Come on!

Come on, Big Chuck.
Climb with us.

Come on!

Really, Chuck!
Those pants are too small.

Pop! Rip!

Oh!

Yay, Big Chuck!
Now you can play with us.